This book belongs to

_____

CLARKSON POTTER is a trademark and POTTER
with colophon is a registered trademark of
Penguin Random House LLC

Inspired by Wonder by R.J. Palacio, copyright
© 2012 by R.J. Palacio

Originally published by Alfred A. Knopf, an imprint
of Random House Children's Books, a division of
Penguin Random House LLC, New York

Selected material originally appeared in Wonder,
by R.J. Palacio, copyright © 2012 by R.J. Palacio;
The Julian Chapter by R.J. Palacio, copyright
© 2014 by R.J. Palacio; 365 Days of Wonder
by R.J. Palacio, copyright © 2014 by R.J. Palacio;
Pluto by R.J. Palacio, copyright © 2015 by
R.J. Palacio

ISBN 978-1-5247-5942-1

Printed in China

Art by Tad Carpenter and Vaughn Fender
Art and logo type copyright © 2012, 2017
by R.J. Palacio and Random House
Children's Books

First Edition
10 9 8 7 6 5 4 3 2 1

FRIENDS OF
★
WONDER

onewarmcoat.org
freerice.com
wish.org
welcomhomeblog.com
serve.gov
sendkidstheworld.com
goodwill.org
stjude.org
operationsmile.org
MyFace
ccakids.com

JANUARY 01

"Kindness can spread from person to person like glitter." —R. J. Palacio

What glitter will you spread this year?

JANUARY 02

What do you think it means to be kind? Write about what you think kindness is. Can you list ten qualities associated with kindness?

1. _____
2. _____
3. _____
4. _____
5. _____
6. _____
7. _____
8. _____
9. _____
10. _____

JANUARY 03

How do you take care of yourself when you are afraid? Do you think you could use that to help someone who is frightened of something?

JANUARY 04

Abraham Joshua Heschel said, "When I was young, I admired clever people. Now that I am old, I admire kind people."

What do you think of this quote? Would you rather be around clever people or kind people?

JANUARY  05

Who is more kind, children or adults?
Why?

JANUARY 06

Next time you win a game, say something kind to the person who lost. Some phrases could include:

You're fun to play with.

I really liked it when you did _____ .

You were a great challenge for me.

Circle one you can imagine saying to an opponent. What else could you say? Write that down below so that you remember it.

JANUARY 07

"Funny how sometimes you worry a lot about something and it turns out to be nothing." —Auggie

What are you worried about? What can you say to yourself to make yourself feel better?

JANUARY 08

Write three Post–it notes of compliments for three people who wouldn't expect it today. If you feel like it, share the notes with those people.

JANUARY  09

Write about a funny moment you had with a family member below. Tonight, ask either that person or a different relative about a funny family story of his or her own.

JANUARY 10

"It's not enough to be friendly. You have to be a friend." —R. J. Palacio

To whom are you a friend? What makes you a good friend to that person?

JANUARY 11

What are you sorry you posted online?

JANUARY 12

Who in your school speaks English as a second language? Write their names and first languages below.

JANUARY 13

Find out how to pronounce a few school words in the first languages of the people in your school. Write them here.

JANUARY 14

Notice someone who is sad today at home or at school. What kinds of things can you say to cheer someone up?

JANUARY 15

Who did you notice? What did you say
or do to make someone feel better
yesterday?

JANUARY 16

Plan a one-minute dance party for tomorrow. Organize it with your teacher or parent for class time or dinnertime. For one minute, play a popular song and encourage everyone to dance. Write down some songs you would play and let your dancers choose from your list.

JANUARY 17

With a family member, look through a local newspaper and find an article about someone doing good for the community. Who was the article about? What did the article say?

JANUARY 18

Think of someone with whom you spend a lot of time. Notice ten nice, little things about that person and write them below.

1. _____
2. _____
3. _____
4. _____
5. _____
6. _____
7. _____
8. _____
9. _____
10. _____

JANUARY 19

Complete this sentence: I am a good friend because _____ .

JANUARY 20

How do you think you can be a better friend?

_____

_____

_____

_____

_____

_____

_____

_____

_____

_____

_____

_____

_____

_____

_____

_____

_____

JANUARY 21

SILENT COMPLIMENT WRITING:
Before dinner tonight, write each family member's name on a different piece of paper. Hand out the sheets randomly so that each person has a piece of paper with someone else's name on it. Have each person write a compliment about that person on his or her sheet. Read them aloud at dinner. How would you compliment each family member?

JANUARY 22

What were the compliments your family members wrote on your notes from last night's dinner?

JANUARY  23

TICKLE TIME:
Choose a sibling, parent, or pet to
tickle today. Who will you tickle? Why?

JANUARY 24

Post flyers in your community that encourage your neighbors to donate old coats and blankets to those in need. Include websites, such as onewarmcoat.org, that help distribute coats and blankets to people in your local area who can use them. What will your flyer say?

JANUARY 25

What was the funniest moment you had this week? Who did you share this moment with? Is it possible to have funny moments alone?

JANUARY 26

Maya Angelou once wrote, "Try to be a rainbow in someone's cloud."

What do you think this means?

JANUARY 27

Were you a rainbow in someone's cloud today? Or did you witness it?
Write about it.

JANUARY 28

"To Daisy, all our faces look alike, as flat and pale as the moon." —Via

What do you think Via means when she says this? That animals don't recognize people's faces, or that, perhaps, they see deeper than our faces?

JANUARY 29

"A teacher affects eternity; he can never tell where his influence stops."
—Henry Adams

Is there a teacher who's affected you in a way that will last your whole life? Have you taught someone something that he or she will remember forever?

JANUARY 30

Offer your company to a younger person today at recess. How can you make that younger person feel good today?

JANUARY  31

What magical invention would you make that could make everyone in your life happier?

FEBRUARY 01

What's an adventure you would like to have with your family? Tomorrow, ask your family members what kind of a family adventure they would like to go on.

FEBRUARY 02

Record the adventures your family members described.

_____
_____
_____
_____
_____
_____
_____
_____
_____
_____
_____
_____
_____
_____
_____
_____
_____
_____
_____

FEBRUARY 03

"Never look down on anybody unless you're helping them up."
—Jesse Jackson

When was the last time you helped someone up?

FEBRUARY  04

Who did you console today? Did you use your words or actions to ease someone's pain?

_____

_____

_____

_____

_____

_____

_____

_____

_____

_____

_____

_____

_____

_____

_____

_____

_____

FEBRUARY 05

Think of an old friend you haven't seen or talked to—or really spent time with—recently. Surprise him or her with a picture. Draw it here first.

FEBRUARY **06**

Write about a time when you helped someone in the last week. Go wide. Perhaps what you did seemed small to you but had a big impact on the other person.

FEBRUARY 07

What was the last compliment you were given? Plan to give five compliments to five different people today. Write them here.

FEBRUARY 08

Who did you compliment? How many smiles did you receive?

FEBRUARY 09

Sign up for freerice.com.

freerice.com is a nonprofit website that supports the United Nations World Food Programme. Its goals are to provide education to everyone for free and to help end world hunger by providing free rice to hungry people.

On its homepage, you will find vocabulary words. For each one you get right, Freerice will donate ten grains of rice to the United Nations World Food Programme.

How many grains of rice did you get today?

FEBRUARY 10

"No act of kindness, no matter how small, is ever wasted." —Aesop

What do you think of this statement?

FEBRUARY 11

"It's not enough to be friendly.
You have to be a friend." —Charlotte

Pick a friend. How do you know this person cares about you?

FEBRUARY 12

Think about someone you love.
Write down all of the things you love
about this person (you'll need this list
tomorrow).

FEBRUARY 13

Create twenty small paper hearts and write twenty things you love about the person you thought of yesterday.
Put your hearts in an envelope or box.
Plan to give it to your special person tomorrow.

FEBRUARY 14

Who did you give your special paper hearts to? How did it feel to surprise someone with love?

_____

_____

_____

_____

_____

_____

_____

_____

_____

_____

_____

_____

_____

_____

_____

_____

FEBRUARY 15

Describe the room you're in right now. How can you make it more beautiful tomorrow?

FEBRUARY 16

Who is your favorite compassionate movie character? Why?

_____

_____

_____

_____

_____

_____

_____

_____

_____

_____

_____

_____

_____

_____

_____

_____

_____

FEBRUARY 17

Today is Random Acts of Kindness Day. What random act of kindness will you do for someone today?

FEBRUARY 18

Did you witness any random acts of kindness yesterday? Think hard! Maybe you saw kindness to a pet, the environment, or the community, if not to an individual person.

FEBRUARY 19

What fascinating new thing have you learned recently? Write it down below and share it with someone tomorrow. Ask that person to share a new fact with you.

FEBRUARY 20

Who did you share with? What did he or she share with you?

FEBRUARY 21

James M. Barrie said, "Those who bring sunshine to the lives of others cannot keep it from themselves."

What do you think he meant by this?

FEBRUARY 22

How can you share sunshine with someone?

_____

_____

_____

_____

_____

_____

_____

_____

_____

_____

_____

_____

_____

_____

_____

_____

_____

_____

_____

FEBRUARY 23

What are ways to keep a friend? See if you can list five below.

1. _____
2. _____
3. _____
4. _____
5. _____

FEBRUARY 24

Oliver Wendell Holmes said, "It is the province of knowledge to speak and it is the privilege of wisdom to listen."

What makes a good listener?

FEBRUARY 25

When was the last time you had fun?
Describe it.

_____

_____

_____

_____

_____

_____

_____

_____

_____

_____

_____

_____

_____

_____

_____

_____

FEBRUARY 26

How can you add fun to someone's life?

FEBRUARY 27

Do you have pajamas that you have out-grown? Donate them to a Goodwill store or another community donation center in your area.

FEBRUARY

Who did you notice and appreciate today? Write down how you acknowledged that person. Maybe it was just by giving a warm smile, or maybe it was another signal or a big gesture.

FEBRUARY 29

Is it a Leap Day? What will you do with your extra day of life this year?

MARCH 01

Edgar A. Guest said, "Let me be a little kinder / Let me be a little blinder / To the faults of those around me."

What annoys you that you will choose to ignore this week?

_____

_____

_____

_____

_____

_____

_____

_____

_____

_____

_____

_____

_____

MARCH 02

Pick up twenty pieces of litter throughout your school day today. What other ways can you make your school community sparkle? List three here.

1. _____

2. _____

3. _____

MARCH 03

Send a video greeting to someone in your family who you don't get to see often. Who will you send it to? What will you say?

MARCH 04

Who do you know who has a kind face? Draw a picture of that person and give it to him or her.

MARCH 05

Who did you give your drawing to? Describe the reaction you received.

MARCH 06

Write down your favorite poem or kindness quote and leave it in a public space. Somewhere on the piece of paper write "This is for you to enjoy, please pass it on." Also, write that favorite poem or kindness quote below.

MARCH 07

"Be silly. Be honest. Be kind."
—Ralph Waldo Emerson

Which were you today?

How have you helped your family this week?

MARCH 09

Notice who is the best listener in your class.
What makes him or her a good listener?
Write down two of those qualities here.

MARCH  10

Take beautiful photos of nature or kids in your school playing at recess (not posed photos). Have a parent or teacher print them and ask if you can sell them and donate your earnings to the St. Jude hospital in your area.

MARCH 11

Small reminders can help others when they need it. Shushing, nudging, and embarrassing someone can be hurtful. What are ways you like to be reminded? List a few below.

MARCH  12

Make a list of your favorite celebrities below.

MARCH 13

Do some research and find out if your favorite celebrities help other people. In what ways do they share their time or money, or put their fame to good use? What did you find out?

MARCH 14

Help someone stay on track if he or she isn't paying attention or doesn't know the rules. What are some gentle ways you can do this?

MARCH 15

Disappointment comes to everyone, but it is not an easy thing to face. What can you say or do to comfort someone who feels disappointment?

_____

_____

_____

_____

_____

_____

_____

_____

_____

_____

_____

_____

_____

_____

_____

MARCH **16**

"The earth laughs in flowers."
—Ralph Waldo Emerson

Today, collect flowers from your garden or make paper flowers. Take them to a local hospital with a note, such as "Thank you for taking care of people," and ask that they be placed at a nurses' station.

MARCH 17

"Kindness is like snow. It beautifies everything it covers." —Kahlil Gibran

Be kind to yourself today. Read a book or poem that you love. What will you read?

MARCH 18

Next time you are with your family at a store, ask a family member to purchase a small item for the person behind you. How might this make that person feel?

MARCH  19

How can you be less wasteful at school or at home? Write down three ways and see if you can do them.

MARCH 20

Eating with others can make people feel connected. What food will you share today?

MARCH 21

Think of an elderly person in your neighborhood.
What are some ways you can help that person?
Write down two below.

MARCH 22

When someone feels that he or she can teach you something you'd like to learn, it makes him or her feel honored. Think about someone in your life who knows how to do something you would like to do. Write a note asking him or her to be your mentor. What would your note say?

MARCH 23

"Don't wait for people to be friendly, show them how." —Anonymous

How can you be a leader in love today?

MARCH 24

Ask a grown-up to help you visit your elderly neighbor to offer a service. Who would you like to visit?

_____

_____

_____

_____

_____

_____

_____

_____

_____

_____

_____

_____

_____

_____

_____

_____

_____

MARCH 25

Who do you have the most fun with?
What do you do together?

MARCH 26

Write the warmest phrase or sentence you heard today. Who said it?

MARCH 27

Describe a thoughtful act you witnessed today.

MARCH  28

Actions like hugs, handshakes, and winks can show affection and friendliness. What are other nonverbal ways to show warmth?

MARCH 29

What actions of affection and friendliness did you witness today? Describe one.

MARCH 30

Audrey Hepburn said, "As you grow older, you will discover that you have two hands, one for helping yourself, the other for helping others."

How have you helped yourself today? How have you helped someone else?

MARCH 31

Where is your favorite place in nature? Think of someone you would like to take to that place. It might be a park or a swimming hole or maybe it's just a beautiful tree near your home.

APRIL 01

Write down some of your family's and friends' favorite jokes or pranks below.

Put the jokes you wrote yesterday on separate index cards or small pieces of paper. Hide them in classroom books or friends' books. Which joke was your favorite? Where will you hide them?

Today, try to spend a day mostly listening to others. Ask questions and just listen. What questions might you ask a family member, friend, or neighbor to show that you care about him or her?

APRIL 04

Today, think about someone who you think about but doesn't live close to you. Who is it? Why might he or she want to hear from you? What might you say to him or her?

APRIL  05

Words are like toothpaste: easy to come out, hard to put back in. Have you ever said something you wish you hadn't?

APRIL 06

Ask a family member what his or her favorite song was when he or she was your age. Then ask the family member to sing or play it for you. As you both listen to it, watch his or her face. Draw what you see.

APRIL 07

What song did your family member share with you yesterday? Did you like watching him or her play or sing it?

_____

_____

_____

_____

_____

_____

_____

_____

_____

_____

_____

_____

_____

_____

_____

_____

APRIL 08

Plan a picnic. Who will you invite? What will you need?

"How beautiful a day can be when kindness touches it." —George Elliston

How can you make today beautiful?

APRIL 10

Natalie's song is about a person whose appearance "confounds" and "astounds." When have you encountered someone who looks different from you?

APRIL 11

Small acts of thoughtfulness can make a difference in a person's day. Today, hold the door open
or keep an elevator door open for someone. If he
or she is a little far behind and begins to rush,
continue to hold it and say, "Don't rush. I'm not in
a hurry." What other small acts can you do to be
thoughtful to others?

APRIL 12

Why is it important to listen to others when they share their thinking?

APRIL 13

Interview your family members about their favorite songs. Make a playlist of their favorite songs. Play it during dinner or family drives. Write the list below.

APRIL 14

Organize a family game night. Make sure you have games everyone would like to play. Write down the highlights of the night that have nothing to do with winning or losing.

APRIL  15

"Kindness is the language which the deaf can hear and the blind can see." —Mark Twain

What do you think this means?

APRIL 16

Which animal do you think most people can learn the most from? Have you ever learned anything from an animal?

APRIL 17

Our reactions can really impact others. Eye rolling, sighing, and crossing arms can be hurtful. What are some other hurtful reactions?

APRIL 18

At school, look out for students and teachers who react with warmth. What warm reactions did you observe?

APRIL 19

"If you truly loved yourself, you could never hurt another." —Buddha

How have you loved yourself today?

APRIL 20

When was the last time you cried? Did anyone make you feel better? At school tomorrow, console someone who looks hurt.

APRIL 21

"My religion is very simple. My religion is kindness." —The Dalai Lama

What do you think this means? If you practice a religion, write down some of the values of kindness that are important to your faith.

APRIL 22

Today is Earth Day. List ten ways you can be kind to the Earth this spring and summer.

1. _____
2. _____
3. _____
4. _____
5. _____
6. _____
7. _____
8. _____
9. _____
10. _____

APRIL 23

It makes others feel appreciated when they are noticed and complimented. What is something you can notice and compliment a cashier, post office worker, or restaurant server the next time you see one?

APRIL 24

What are some things you can say to a young child who is crying? Plan to comfort the next crying child you see.

APRIL  25

Try to get rid of the "me first" mentality. The next time you are offered something (a sharp pencil, a piece of cake, a spot in line), let others go first. How might this feel?

APRIL 26

Rewrite this sentence, filling in the blanks.
Tomorrow I will _____ because
it will make _____ happy.

APRIL 27

Study with a classmate. What would you like to study? Who will be a good study partner?

_____

_____

_____

_____

_____

_____

_____

_____

_____

_____

_____

_____

_____

_____

_____

_____

_____

APRIL 28

"You don't need a reason to help people."
—Charles Dickens

How does that quote inspire you?

APRIL 29

Write about a time when you stood up for a friend who was being teased.

Do you know anyone who isn't feeling well?
Write a get-well card.

MAY 01

Describe a time when you showed sympathy to someone else.

MAY 02

Think of someone in your school—maybe a custodian or a cafeteria worker or an administrator—who strikes you as being underappreciated. Make a snack or a card to give to him or her today.

MAY 03

If you wanted to play a different game than a friend, what kind ways could you tell him or her?

MAY 04

Have you ever been surprised by a stranger's kindness? Leave change in a vending machine today or tape quarters to a parking meter. It will make someone's day.

MAY 05

"Remember that everyone you meet is afraid of something, loves something and has lost something." —H. Jackson Brown Jr.

What do you think of this quote?

What are you afraid of?

MAY 07

What is something you love?

MAY 08

What is something you lost?

MAY 09

"A bit of fragrance clings to the hand that gives flowers." —Chinese proverb

What do you think this phrase means?

MAY 10

Have you ever been given a surprise note? Leave a surprise note in someone's mailbox today. Draft it here.

SOME WORDS AND ACTIONS OF KINDNESS ARE:

WORDS ───────────────

good morning   good night
you go first   thank you
it's okay, take your time   please

ACTIONS ───────────────

smiling   making you breakfast, lunch, dinner
hugging asking others questions
listening   watering plants

*AND SO MANY MORE!

MAY 11

What's your favorite poem? Copy it below.

MAY 12

Share your poem with someone and ask that person what his or her favorite poem is.

MAY 13

When was the last time you got a great hug? Give a
hug coupon to someone today.

★ ★ ★

MAY 14

Bury a treasure box with old toys in a playground
Then give a treasure map to some children to find it.
What would you bury? How might they feel to find it?

MAY 15

Do you like playing with chalk or bubbles? Leave them on someone's doorstep today with a note saying "Enjoy!"

MAY 16

Practice conserving water: Turn off the water while brushing your teeth. What else can you and your family do to be kind to the Earth?

MAY 17

"Courage. Kindness. Friendship. Character. These are the qualities that define us as human beings, and propel us, on occasion, to greatness."
—Mr. Tushman, from *Wonder*

Do you agree?

MAY 18

Create a jar of love notes for your mother or father. Write the things you love on pieces of paper and put them in.

MAY 19

Write about a time when someone felt happy for you.

_____

_____

_____

_____

_____

_____

_____

_____

_____

_____

_____

_____

_____

_____

_____

_____

_____

MAY 20

Write about a time when you felt happy for someone else.

_____

_____

_____

_____

_____

_____

_____

_____

_____

_____

_____

_____

_____

_____

_____

_____

_____

_____

MAY

"The true measure of an individual is how he treats
a person who can do him absolutely no good."
—Ann Landers

What do you think this means?

MAY 22

How can you relate the quote from yesterday to your own life?

MAY 23

"A multitude of small delights constitute happiness." —Charles Baudelaire

What small delights did you collect today?

MAY 24

In *Shingaling, A Wonder Story*, Charlotte talks about "a blind old man who played the accordion on Main Street," who she used to see on her way to school. She finds out that he was a veteran. He has a story to tell.

Are there homeless people in your area who have stories to tell? Keep extra bottles of water and snack bars in your book bag. Hand them out when you see someone who needs them. How does it make you feel when you do this?

MAY 25

Do you feel and show concern for everyone in the same way? Why or why not?

MAY 26

Do you like playing with play dough?
Make some play dough for a preschool
class using the recipe below.

INGREDIENTS

Large mixing bowl ✳ 1 cup water
food coloring ✳ 4 cups flour
1 ½ cups of salt
2 to 4 tablespoons of cooking oil (such as canola)

INSTRUCTIONS

Pour water into a large mixing bowl.

Next, add food coloring in a shade of your choice.
Once you add the food coloring to the water, stir
well.

play dough

Add the dry ingredients (flour and salt) to the
mix. You can stir a little at this point to begin
blending the ingredients.

Next add 2 to 4 tablespoons of oil. You can add
more oil later if the mix seems too dry. Oil is the
secret to keeping this "no cooking required"
recipe soft! If you don't add enough oil, the mix
will be very crumbly.

Knead the ingredients together until a soft
dough is formed.

MAY 27

Have you ever found a penny on the sidewalk? Some people think that finding a heads-up penny will bring them good luck. Sprinkle heads-up pennies on the sidewalk for others to find.

MAY 28

"Be kind, for everyone you meet is fighting a hard battle." —Ian Maclaren

What do you battle that others cannot see?

MAY 29

What are your artistic talents? Use the space below to let your talents shine. Next time you see someone create a drawing or piece of art, compliment the piece.

MAY 30

Do a chore for someone without him or her knowing. What will you do? Who will you do it for?

MAY 31

Write an email to a family member you haven't seen in a while. Who will you write to? What will you say?

JUNE 01

Are there many plants in classrooms at your school? Offer to water them today.

JUNE  02

Do you have any toys, coloring books, or crayons that you never use? Ask a family member if you can donate them to your school or to a children's hospital today.

JUNE 03

Write kind chalk messages on the streets in your neighborhood. What are some phrases you can write?

JUNE 04

"If you have good thoughts they will shine out of your face like sunbeams and you will always look lovely." —Roald Dahl

Draw what your face looks like when you have good thoughts.

JUNE 05

JUNE 06

In your next gym class or sport you play, shout only encouraging phrases to your classmates. What could you say to encourage them?

JUNE 07

What would you do if you found twenty dollars at your school?

JUNE

"What this world needs is a new kind of army—
the army of the kind." —Cleveland Amory

Who is in your army of the kind?

JUNE  09

"The more I wonder, the more I love."
—Alice Walker

What is something you wonder?

JUNE  10

Who do you want to know a bit better? What three things can you ask him or her to get to know this person?

JUNE 11

"Sometimes you don't have to mean to hurt someone." —R. J. Palacio

Be careful with your words today.

JUNE 12

Plan to play a game with someone you don't usually play with. Think about how you will initiate this below.

JUNE **13**

PAY IT FORWARD:
Put five dollars in an envelope with a note that reads "Do something good with this." Leave the envelope in a public place. What would you do if you found that envelope?

JUNE 14

"Fall seven times. Stand up eight."
—Japanese proverb

When was the last time you helped someone stand up?

JUNE 15

"Let us always meet each other with a smile."
—Mother Teresa

How many smiles can you give out today?

JUNE 16

Partner with a friend to draw colorful pictures and send them to colorasmile.org, which sends your drawings to senior citizens and troops overseas. Practice your sketch below.

JUNE 17

"Your deeds are your monuments."
—Egyptian inscription

Draw your monument below.

JUNE 18

"Kindness is a melody everyone can sing along to."
—Unknown

What do you think this means?

JUNE 19

Who might need the close parking spaces at the grocery store? Next time you go to the grocery store, ask your parent to park farther away and save the close space for others who might need it.

JUNE 20

When was the last time you played at a park? Next time you go, try to leave the space better than the way you found it. Write down some ways you can do that.

JUNE 21

"Kindness, like a boomerang, always returns."
—Unknown

What does this mean to you?

JUNE 22

What does your room or another space in your house look like today? Draw it below.

JUNE 23

Tidy up your room or another part of the house without being asked to do so. Draw it below.

JUNE 24

"Small minds discuss people. Average minds discuss events. Great minds discuss ideas."
—Eleanor Roosevelt

What do you think this means?

_____

_____

_____

_____

_____

_____

_____

_____

_____

_____

_____

_____

_____

_____

JUNE 25

Look at your answer from yesterday. How will you change the conversation today?

JUNE 26

What is your favorite book? Why?

JUNE 27

"The mind is everything. What you think, you become." —Anonymous

What do you want to be?

JUNE 28

When was the last time someone hugged you?

JUNE 29

Write about a time when you shared and played fairly with a friend.

JUNE 30

Which house in your neighborhood is beautifully decorated? Draw a picture of it and write "Thank you for giving us something beautiful to look at every day." Practice the picture below.

JULY 01

"There are always flowers for those who want to see them." —Henri Matisse

Notice the flowers in your life today.

JULY 02

Is there something you're sorry you said? What is it?

JULY 03

"Act with kindness, but do not expect gratitude."
—Confucius

Do something today without expecting a thank you.

JULY 04

"In a gentle way, you can shake the world."
—Mahatma Gandhi

In what ways can you be gentle?

JULY 05

Some jobs are harder than others. Leave a note or drawing on your garbage cans for the sanitation workers to find. What could you draw or write that might make them smile?

JULY 06

Do you like playing in the rain? Write about an adventure you had in the rain. Next time it rains, ask a family member to help you dry the slides at a local park afterward.

JULY 07

When was the last time you said thank you to someone?

JULY **08**

Surprise your parents today. Wash your family car before anyone gets up to go anywhere. What will you need to do to have everything ready to do a speedy job?

JULY 09

Leave a happy note in your bathroom for someone to find. What can you write on the bathroom note?

JULY 10

"Kindness makes you the most beautiful person in the world no matter what you look like." —Unknown

Look out for beautiful people today. They are everywhere.

JULY 11

Where did you see beautiful people? What made them so?

JULY 12

Who inspires you? Write down why.

JULY 13

Write a note to the person who inspires you and give it to him or her.

JULY 14

Do a family member's chore for him or her today.
If he or she asks why, just say "No reason. I just
wanted to help." What will you do?

JULY 15

What flowers are growing in your garden? Draw the flowers below. Leave one on your neighbor's doorstep.

JULY 16

Clean out your closet today. What things did you
find that you can give away? Who can use them?

JULY 17

"Throw kindness around like confetti."
—Unknown

How will you sprinkle love today?

JULY 18

Who in your life really trusts you? How do you know?

JULY 19

Plan a trading party with close friends. Bring clothing and toys and plan an exchange. Who will you invite? What will you bring? Why?

JULY 20

Who do you miss? Write an "I miss you"
message and send it to someone today.
Draft your note below.

JULY 21

Write about a time you helped someone you didn't know.

JULY 22

Look around your neighborhood. Is anyone working in the heat? Freeze water bottles and hand them out to people who look hot!

JULY 23

Write a thank-you letter to someone who is not expecting it. Who will you write to? What will you say?

JULY 24

"What wisdom can you find that is greater than kindness?" —Jean-Jacques Rousseau

What do you think?

JULY 25

When was the last time you were given a balloon? Next time you're at a party store, buy balloons and hand them out to kids you see in town and in parks.

JULY  26

In your own words, define what you think it means to be kind.

JULY 27

When have you done something kind for someone else?

JULY 28

What character in a book do you think is kind? Why?

JULY 29

Think about the people in your family. Who do you think is kind? Why do you think so?

JULY

Today, write a note to a family member that lists all of the kind things he or she has said or done. The title of the note can be *YOU ARE KIND* or **KINDNESS I NOTICED IN YOU.**

SOME WORDS AND ACTIONS OF KINDNESS ARE:

WORDS

good morning   good night
you go first   thank you
it's okay, take your time   please

ACTIONS

smiling   making you breakfast, lunch, dinner
hugging asking others questions
listening   watering plants

*AND SO MANY MORE!

JULY 31

Write about what you wrote yesterday. Who did you give it to? How did your kindness note make your family member feel?

_____

_____

_____

_____

_____

_____

_____

_____

_____

_____

_____

_____

_____

_____

_____

AUGUST **01**

Where did you see a stranger be kind to someone today?

AUGUST 02

Who was the last person to make you feel
_____ ? Fill in the blank from the
list of words below. Write about what he
or she did to make you feel that way.

Loved ✺ Appreciated ✺ Proud
Respected ✺ Confident ✺ Giddy

AUGUST 03

Write your favorite joke below. Who told you the joke? Why do you like it?

AUGUST 04

Tell the joke to someone else. Did that person laugh? If so, how did that make you feel?

AUGUST 05

Surprise someone with a gift. Think about the person and the gift. Why will he or she like it?

AUGUST 06

How did it feel to surprise that person yesterday?

AUGUST **07**

Have you ever seen a friend be kind to
someone other than you? Write about it.

AUGUST 08

Create a human knot with friends today. Reach out your hands and clasp them together with someone in front of you. Then, without letting go, try to untangle the human knot. Do you think this will be easy? Why or why not?

AUGUST 09

Do you think animals are kind? If so, how?

AUGUST 10

Do you want someone to share something with you? Is it tangible or intangible?

AUGUST 11

Have you ever seen an adult be kind to another adult? Write about it.

AUGUST 12

Who do you think is more thoughtful:
children or adults? Why?

AUGUST 13

What is your most valued toy? Would you ever give it away to someone who wanted it? Explain.

_____

_____

_____

_____

_____

_____

_____

_____

_____

_____

_____

_____

AUGUST 14

Think about words that comfort people.
List ten comforting words below.

1. _____
2. _____
3. _____
4. _____
5. _____
6. _____
7. _____
8. _____
9. _____
10. _____

AUGUST 15

Choose a book you loved to donate to a friend in the neighborhood. Write a note about why you loved the book and why you want to share it below. Give it to someone tomorrow.

AUGUST 16

Who did you share your book with? How did he or she react?

_____

_____

_____

_____

_____

_____

_____

_____

_____

_____

_____

_____

_____

_____

_____

_____

AUGUST 17

"Kind words can be short and easy to spread, but their echoes are truly endless."
—Mark Twain

What kind words will you never forget?

AUGUST 18

Make it a habit not to sit down at a table until you know there is a seat for everyone. When was the last time you gathered at a table with others? What did you do: eat, play, or think?

AUGUST 19

What is something you have to offer at a dinner party? Flowers? Music? Food? Jokes? Below, write what you have to bring to the table.

AUGUST 20

Ask your family to be gentle to the Earth today. Instead of getting into a car, walk, ride a bike, or skip to the places you need to go to. What other ways can you be kind to the Earth?

AUGUST 21

Make a list of the ways you can help your neighbors below (watering plants, feeding pets, etc.).

AUGUST 22

Visit a neighbor (or a few neighbors!) and show them your list. How did it feel to offer your time to someone?

AUGUST  23

Interview your family members about their favorite animals, songs, etc. What are the things they love?

AUGUST 24

"When given the choice of being right or being kind, choose kind."
—Dr. Wayne W. Dyer

Does this quote remind you of anytime in your life? Think for a few minutes and then write about that time.

AUGUST 25

SMILE MISSION:
Tomorrow, smile at everyone you see for the entire day. How do you think this might make others feel?

_____

_____

_____

_____

_____

_____

_____

_____

_____

_____

_____

_____

_____

_____

AUGUST 26

How many smiles did you get in return yesterday? How did that make you feel?

AUGUST 27

What ways can you give your time to others? Brainstorm here.

AUGUST 28

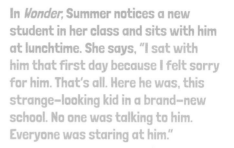

In *Wonder*, Summer notices a new student in her class and sits with him at lunchtime. She says, "I sat with him that first day because I felt sorry for him. That's all. Here he was, this strange-looking kid in a brand-new school. No one was talking to him. Everyone was staring at him."

Have you ever been a new student at a school? Or, do you know any new students?

AUGUST 29

Make a pledge to be a friend to a new student in your class this year. What can you do to make this person feel welcome and comfortable at your school?

AUGUST 30

What school supplies do you think every child needs? Donate a set of school supplies to a local Goodwill, church, or school.

AUGUST **31**

"If you can't think of anything nice to say,
you're not thinking hard enough."
—Kid President

What kind words will you say today?

SEPTEMBER 01

What does the word *giving* mean?

SEPTEMBER 02

Plan to give someone something of yours tomorrow. What will you give? Who will you give it to?

SEPTEMBER 03

What did you give? How did the recipient of the gift react?

SEPTEMBER **04**

Think of chores that you usually have to be asked to do. Write them below. Tomorrow, do one of your chores without being asked.

SEPTEMBER 05

What chore did you do without being asked? How did it feel?

SEPTEMBER 06

"There is nothing more truly artistic than to love people."
—Vincent van Gogh

What does this quote mean to you?

SEPTEMBER 07

People like to be greeted by name. Today, learn the names of people you see every day at school. It could be the security guards, custodians, school office staff, bus driver. Ask them their names and tell them your name.

SEPTEMBER **08**

Whose names did you learn yesterday? Next time you see them, greet them by name and remind them of yours if they've forgotten it.

SEPTEMBER 09

Who was the most helpful in the classroom yesterday? Write an "I noticed" note to give to that person tomorrow. What will the note say? Write your first draft below.

SOME WORDS AND ACTIONS OF KINDNESS ARE:

WORDS

good morning   good night
you go first   thank you
it's okay, take your time   please

ACTIONS

smiling   making you breakfast, lunch, dinner
hugging   asking others questions
listening   watering plants

*AND SO MANY MORE!

SEPTEMBER 10

Give your note to the helpful classmate. How did he or she react?

SEPTEMBER 11

Draw a picture of a firefighter doing something helpful for your community. Ask a family member if you can give it to a firehouse today.

SEPTEMBER 12

"We may never truly know the reach of an act of kindness or the mark that it leaves on a life." —Topaz

Who has been kind to you and may not know it?

SEPTEMBER 13

Write a note to the person you wrote about yesterday. You can decide later if you want to share the note with that person.

SEPTEMBER **14**

What are ways you show that you're sorry?

SEPTEMBER **15**

Good friends spring into action when a person needs help. Have you ever had a friend spring into action to help when you needed it? Explain what happened.

SEPTEMBER **16**

"Every day may not be glorious, but there's something glorious in every day." —Precept in *365 Days of Wonder*

Do you agree? Why or why not?

SEPTEMBER 17

Ask your parents about their childhoods. What are some of their favorite memories?

SEPTEMBER 18

Write a recipe of a good friend below.
(For example: ½ teaspoon of honesty,
¾ tablespoons of humor, etc.)

SEPTEMBER 19

Write a recipe for cookies or cupcakes below. Make these treats for each member of your classroom, family, or neighbor sometime this week.

SEPTEMBER 20

"What is beautiful is good. And who is good, shall also be beautiful."
—Sappho

Draw something that only you think is beautiful.

SEPTEMBER 21

"Always be mindful of the kindness and not the faults of others."
—Buddha

Look out for the good in people today. What did you find?

SEPTEMBER 22

Write a list of compliments people have given you below. Tomorrow, try to compliment at least five people.

SEPTEMBER 23

Who did you compliment? What did you say? How did it feel?

SEPTEMBER **24**

You don't always need words to make others feel good. Sometimes our body language can make people feel special. Notice people that do the following today:

____ ⚑ Smile

____ ⚑ Greet others when they walk into the room

____ ⚑ Make eye contact when someone is talking

____ ⚑ High-five

____ ⚑ Hold hands

____ ⚑ Rub the back of someone who is sad

SEPTEMBER 25

Who did you notice? What did you see? Which one will you try tomorrow?

SEPTEMBER 26

What did you try yesterday? How did it go? Draw a picture of what you did below.

SEPTEMBER 27

"Forget injuries, never forget kindnesses." —Confucius

What injury will you choose to forget today?

SEPTEMBER 28

What kindness will you never forget?

SEPTEMBER 29

What kindness did you give that someone may never forget?

SEPTEMBER 30

Describe your recess time below. Who do you play with? What do you play?

OCTOBER 01

Spend a recess noticing others. Invite someone who is alone to play with you, or ask to play a game he or she likes.

OCTOBER 02

How did it go yesterday? Who did you notice needed a friend? How did it feel to be a friend to someone who needed one?

OCTOBER 03

Buy seeds to plant flowers or trees. Ask friends to find a place to plant the seeds in your neighborhood. Draw your favorite flowers and trees.

OCTOBER 04

Ashleigh Brilliant, a cartoonist, said, "Be kind to unkind people. They need it the most."

What do you think that means?

OCTOBER 05

"Olivia reminds me of a bird sometimes, how her feathers get all ruffled when she's mad. And when she's fragile like this, she's a little lost bird looking for its nest. So I give her my wing to hide under."
—R. J. Palacio

Who have you ever given a "wing to hide under" or comforted when he or she was mad/sad? Write about it.

OCTOBER 06

When was the last time you were comforted by someone? Who comforted you? What did he or she do?

OCTOBER 07

Write a thank-you note or draw a picture of your neighborhood for your mail carrier and leave it in your mailbox. Draft the note or sketch the drawing below.

OCTOBER 08

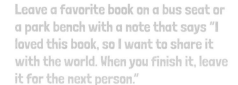

DO A PAY-IT-FORWARD ACTION:
Leave a favorite book on a bus seat or a park bench with a note that says "I loved this book, so I want to share it with the world. When you finish it, leave it for the next person."

OCTOBER 09

Is there someone older in your life that you feel might be lonely? Spend a day asking him or her questions about life at your age. What might you want to know?

OCTOBER 10

In *Wonder*, Mr. Tushman says, "Kinder than is necessary." He repeated, "What a marvelous line, isn't it? Kinder than is necessary. Because it's not enough to be kind. One should be kinder than needed." What does it mean to be "kinder than necessary"?

_____

_____

_____

_____

_____

_____

_____

_____

_____

_____

_____

OCTOBER 11

What stories, poems, or songs did you love to hear when you were little? List them below. Ask a teacher of a younger grade level if you can share a story with a younger student. He or she can act it out as you read or just listen. What stories might a younger student love?

_____

_____

_____

_____

_____

_____

_____

_____

_____

_____

_____

_____

_____

_____

OCTOBER 12

HELP MAKE A CHILD'S DREAM COME TRUE:
With a grown-up, visit wish.org (the Make-
A-Wish Foundation website). Choose a wish
to help make come true. Which wish stands
out to you?

OCTOBER 13

Invent your own holiday. It could be "Mom Appreciation Day" or "Teacher Day" or "Best Friend Day"—put it on the calendar. Celebrate it every year! Who would you create a holiday for?

OCTOBER 14

Put a gratitude box in your home or classroom, with a set of notes next to it. Encourage family members or classmates to put a note in the box when they feel grateful for something. Read the notes each week or each month. Start the box with notes from you. What are you grateful for?

OCTOBER 15

Spend a day loving an animal. You can spend the day with your own pet, a friend's pet, or researching a way to help an animal—rescue mission online. Which animal would you spend a day loving?

OCTOBER 16

Keep an umbrella in your book bag. Share it with a stranger on a rainy day. How might an umbrella be a symbol for caring?

OCTOBER 17

Change the conversation: If you hear someone gossiping about someone, add something you think is positive about that person. How might that help to stop gossip?

OCTOBER 18

Enlist a friend to help survey your classmates' favorite things (animals, ice cream flavors, anything you can think of). Keep the list where you and your friend can access it and draw a picture or write a poem about it. You could also donate the real thing to a classmate when they least expect it. What are some of your friends' favorites?

OCTOBER 19

When was the last time someone really listened to you? Write about it.

OCTOBER 20

Describe a time when you showed sympathy to someone else.

_____

_____

_____

_____

_____

_____

_____

_____

_____

_____

_____

_____

_____

_____

_____

_____

_____

OCTOBER 21

What are good manners? Who do you know who has good manners?

OCTOBER 22

Words can be helpful or hurtful. Today, listen for helpful words and write them below as you hear them.

OCTOBER 23

What helpful words did you say to others today?

OCTOBER 24

LITTER ALERT DAY:
Be on the alert for something you can pick up and throw away on your way to school, in your classroom, in the hallways, in the recess yard, etc. Watch to see if others start picking up litter when they see you doing it.

OCTOBER 25

Did you make your world more beautiful by picking up litter throughout the day yesterday? Did you notice anyone start to do the same?

OCTOBER 26

Tomorrow, ask your friend to help you write a surprise note to your teacher. At lunch, ask other classmates to write something they learned from your teacher on the note. What is something you recently learned?

OCTOBER 27

Did you give the note to your teacher? How did he or she react? How did it make you and your friend feel?

OCTOBER 28

Be good to yourself. What will you do to make yourself healthier, either in mind, body, or spirit? You can exercise, eat healthful food, close your eyes and take ten deep breaths, listen and dance to your favorite song, draw a picture of a place you love—you choose! It's your day. What will you do?

OCTOBER 29

What did you do to be good to yourself yesterday?

OCTOBER 30

Say "yes" today. If a classmate asks to play or a family member asks for help, say yes. You might make someone's day.

OCTOBER 31

How many times did you say "yes" yesterday?

NOVEMBER 01

Who do you know who has a kind heart? Write him or her a note on a paper heart. Hand it out when that person will least expect it.

SOME WORDS AND ACTIONS OF KINDNESS ARE:

WORDS ————————

good morning   good night
you go first   thank you
it's okay, take your time   please

ACTIONS ————————

smiling   making you breakfast, lunch, dinner
hugging   asking others questions
listening   watering plants

AND SO MANY MORE!

NOVEMBER 02

"Kindness is the root of all good things." —Unknown

Where does kindness exist in nature?

NOVEMBER 03

Write a thank-you card for your teacher. Why are you thankful for him or her?

NOVEMBER 04

Take a nature walk. Do you see gentleness, kindness, or selflessness in nature? Draw what you see.

NOVEMBER 05

Plants are living things. Some people believe that talking to them with love helps them grow. Write about all of the encouraging things you can say to a plant in your home or near your home.

Some examples can be: "I think you are beautiful and I want you to grow" or "Thank you for the oxygen you give our family."

NOVEMBER 06

Water the plants inside your home or outside your home. Read your list of positive words and sentences as you water your plants. How did it feel to do this? Do you think it's important to be kind to plants? Why or why not?

NOVEMBER 07

Set the table for breakfast, lunch, or dinner and write a note as a place setting for each person in your family. What will you say to each person?

NOVEMBER 08

Create a box for your home or classroom that says "The Most Beautiful Thing I Saw Today" and encourage people to fill it with notes or drawings. Draw the most beautiful thing you saw today.

NOVEMBER 09

Ask your older family members if they knew anyone who was ever in a war. Listen as they speak. Who will you talk to?

NOVEMBER 10

Visit welcomehomeblog.com to watch surprise military homecomings. Describe how it might feel to see your friends, family, or pets after a long time away from them.

NOVEMBER 11

Make paper flowers, or bring real flowers, to a local veterans' office. What could you write on your paper flowers?

NOVEMBER 12

Give someone a chance to help you today. What do you need help with? Who can you ask for help today?

NOVEMBER 13

Today is World Kindness Day! Celebrate by donating books, food, or clothes to those in need.

NOVEMBER 14

A QUICK WRITE:
What words come to mind when you hear the word *love*? Below, write as many words as you can as quickly as you can.

NOVEMBER 15

Be kind to yourself today, and if someone is doing something that hurts you,
let that person know. How will you tell
him or her?

NOVEMBER 16

Write about a chore that someone in your family (or who helps your family, like a babysitter) does that you know he or she does not enjoy (doing the dishes, taking out the garbage, cleaning a pet's tank/litter box, folding laundry, etc.). Tomorrow, surprise your family member by doing the chore for him or her.

NOVEMBER 17

What chore did you take on for some- one else yesterday? How did it feel to surprise that person? How do you think the chore made him or her feel?

NOVEMBER 18

When was the last time someone for-
gave you?

NOVEMBER 19

Tomorrow, go up to somebody you don't usually talk to and strike up a conversation. What are some conversation starters that might be comfortable ways for you to engage someone?

NOVEMBER 20

How did it go? Who did you invite to play with or spend time with? How did it feel?

NOVEMBER 21

Put a surprise note in your parent's briefcase or a sibling's lunch box. Who will you write to? What will you write?

NOVEMBER 22

It doesn't take a lot to make someone feel good by simply paying them a compliment. Is there someone you can praise today?

NOVEMBER 23

Tomorrow, ask your teacher or principal if you can start a monthlong schoolwide holiday toy drive. Decorate a box with phrases that will encourage children to give their old toys to local children in need. What will your box say?

NOVEMBER 24

How did it go? Write a note that you can read to other classrooms about the drive.

NOVEMBER 25

"Kindness can spread from person to person like glitter." —Mr. Browne

When was the last time you saw kindness spread?

NOVEMBER 26

Make a change jar. Start by putting in whatever change you can find around the house and ask family members to donate. How much change do you think you can collect in a month? What or who would you donate your change to?

NOVEMBER 27

Go to serve.gov, a website with local volunteer opportunities. You need to enter key words and your zip code to get started. What key words will help you find opportunities that are right for you? Some words may be *tutoring* or *coaching*, for example. List some of your key words below.

NOVEMBER 28

The Dalai Lama said, "If you want others to be happy, practice compassion. If you want to be happy, practice compassion."

Who in your life is compassionate?

NOVEMBER 29

Write a note or an email to a family member who you don't get to see much. Ask him or her questions about what his or her life is like. Who will you write to? What will you ask?

NOVEMBER 30

Go through your closet and put the clothes and shoes you've outgrown or will not wear in a bag. Donate it to a local homeless shelter. List the items you put in the bag.

DECEMBER 01

Ask two quiet classmates about themselves. Below, write a few conversation-starter questions or think of an action that will help make them feel more comfortable.

DECEMBER 02

What do you have in common with the two quiet classmates you talked to yesterday?

DECEMBER 03

"A warm smile is the universal language of kindness."
—William Arthur Ward

Smile at ten new people today.

DECEMBER 04

Next time someone in your family gets coffee or tea, ask him or her to buy a coffee for the person behind you. How do you think this will make the other person feel?

DECEMBER 05

Write down as many words as you can to say you're sorry.

DECEMBER 06

Make special note of the students who have birthdays during the summer when school is not in session. Surprise them on a random schoolday with a summer birthday crown.

DECEMBER 07

In *The Julian Chapter, A Wonder Story*, Granmère shares a sad story about her childhood that her family had never heard before. When asked why, she says, "I do not like to dwell on the past. Life is ahead of us. If we spend too much time looking backward, we can't see where we are going." What do you think she means by that? Do you agree with her?

DECEMBER 08

Today, call an older relative and ask him or her to tell you a story about his or her childhood that you haven't heard before. Write about it here.

DECEMBER 09

Start making a gift for someone that you will give out this holiday. What will you make? Who will you give it to?

DECEMBER 10

"Neither genius, fame, nor love show the greatness of the soul. Only kindness can do that."
—Jean-Baptiste Henri Lacordaire

How did you show your greatness today?

DECEMBER 11

Who do you miss? A friend you met over the summer? A relative who lives far away? A pet that died? Write that animal a letter.

DECEMBER 12

If you could write a letter to anyone who ever lived, who would it be and what would it say?

DECEMBER 13

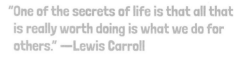

"One of the secrets of life is that all that is really worth doing is what we do for others." —Lewis Carroll

Who in your life puts others before himself or herself?

DECEMBER 14

Many of the elderly have to spend holidays in hospitals. Brainstorm some kind things you can do to make these people feel better this holiday season.

DECEMBER 15

Ask a grown-up to help you with something from yesterday's list. What would you like to do? When will you do it?

DECEMBER 16

ZERO TECHNOLOGY DAY:
Ask your family to spend an entire day
without phones, computers, tablets,
video games, etc. Try to be together and
talk to one another, read together, or
play a game together.

DECEMBER 17

How did your Zero Technology Day go? Write about it.

DECEMBER 18

"Kindness is like snow; it beautifies everything." —Kahlil Gibran

What can you make that's beautiful?

DECEMBER **19**

Ask one of the teachers of the grade younger than yours if there is a lonely student you can volunteer to spend time with during lunch or recess. Brainstorm games you can play with him or her.

DECEMBER 20

Check in on the holiday toy drive. If you weren't able to collect toys from school, ask friends to come over with old toys and wrap them together. Plan to donate them to a homeless shelter or hospital. How is the toy drive going?

DECEMBER 21

Interview the people in your family about their favorite songs, movies, plays, books, and anything else they like. Write down each one's favorites on a separate index card. Then organize a family charade night.

DECEMBER 22

What television shows or movies do you enjoy watching with family members? Plan a movie night. Turn off phones, make popcorn, and create a cozy space.

DECEMBER 23

Send five postcards or notes to kids around the world who are battling illness. Use this site to help: sendkidstheworld.com.

What might be some encouraging words and funny jokes you would write?

DECEMBER 24

Make a "Gifts Money Can't Buy" list and post it in your kitchen. Attach a pen and ask your family members to add to it. What is on your list?

DECEMBER 25

Write thank-you notes to five people today. Who will you write to? Why did you choose them?

DECEMBER 26

Make sandwiches out of leftovers. Ask a grown-up to help you donate them to a local soup kitchen or homeless shelter.

DECEMBER 27

Draw a picture of a special memory you have with a family member. Leave it somewhere he or she will see it. What is a special memory you have? Practice the drawing below.

DECEMBER 28

Spend the day playing a game that a friend or sibling likes to play. What games might they want you to play?

DECEMBER 29

"Kindness can become its own motive.
We are made kind by being kind."
—Eric Hoffer

Have you done something today that's
made you a kinder person?

DECEMBER 30

Who made your life better this year with his or her kindness, generosity, time, or love? Make a list.

DECEMBER 31

Write thank-you letters to the people who made a difference in your life this year. Send them today.